P9-CJD-008

Will You Take Care of Me?

Will You Take Care of Me?

MARGARET PARK BRIDGES
illustrated by MELISSA SWEET

Morrow Junior Books
New York

To my parents with gratitude,
for never expecting any.
—M.P.B.

To my mom, who taught me how to make everything from paper dolls
to a pretty good pie crust. Thanks for taking care of me.
—M.S.

Watercolors were used for the full-color illustrations.
The text type is 28-point Pixie.

Text copyright © 1998 by Margaret Park Bridges
Illustrations copyright © 1998 by Melissa Sweet

Published by Morrow Junior Books
a division of William Morrow and Company, Inc.
1350 Avenue of the Americas, New York, NY 10019
www.williammorrow.com

Printed in Hong Kong by South China Printing Company (1988) Ltd.

10 9 8 7 6 5 4 3

Library of Congress Cataloging-in-Publication Data
Bridges, Margaret Park.
Will you take care of me?/Margaret Park Bridges;
illustrated by Melissa Sweet.
p. cm.
Summary: As a child imagines becoming a tree, a house, a book, a teddy bear,
and more, Mommy tells how she will continue to love and care for her "little one."
ISBN 0-688-15194-9 (trade)—ISBN 0-688-15195-7 (library)
[1. Mother and child—Fiction.] I. Sweet, Melissa, ill. II. Title
PZ7.B7619Wi 1998
[E]—dc21 97-32917 CIP AC

Time to go home, little one.

Will I *always* be little, Mama?

Every day you grow bigger and bigger, my love!

But when I'm big, will you still
take care of me?

Of course. As long as I can make your life
better and help you grow.

What about when I'm all grown up?

No matter how you change,
I'll always want to help.

But what if I became...an apple tree?
Would you still take care of me?

Well! If you were an apple tree...
I'd pluck your fruit and make
warm, sweet applesauce.

What if I turned into a field
of flowers?

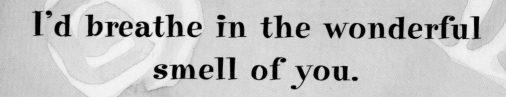

I'd breathe in the wonderful smell of you.

What if I became a bicycle?

I'd pump up your tires so you could ride far away and come back *fast*.

What if I turned into a house?

I'd wash all your windows
so you could see the world.

What if I became a bar of soap?

I'd hold you tight
so you wouldn't slip away.

SOAP

What if I turned into a picture book?

You'd be too good to put down!

What if I turned into a lightbulb?

I'd put you in a lamp
to light up my nights.

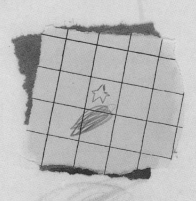

What if I became a bed?

I'd dress you up in a bright patchwork quilt and feather pillows.

What if I turned into a teddy bear?

I'd mend your ragged seams and hug you when I was lonely.

What if I became a star?

I would close my eyes and
make a wish on you.

But what would you wish?

I'd wish for all your wishes
to come true.

What if I became a grown-up and
could do everything myself?

I'd still give you a hug whenever you needed one.

What if I turned back into a baby?
Would you take care of me
all over again?

Of course, little one! I'd feed you and change you and rock you to sleep every night.

And I'll *always* love you

just as much as I do today.